Osman Castle Hooper

**The Harrison Log Cabin Song Book of 1840**

Revised for the Campaign of 1888

Osman Castle Hooper

**The Harrison Log Cabin Song Book of 1840**
*Revised for the Campaign of 1888*

ISBN/EAN: 9783337119836

Printed in Europe, USA, Canada, Australia, Japan

Cover: Foto ©Andreas Hilbeck / pixelio.de

More available books at **www.hansebooks.com**

# THE HARRISON

1840

1888

# LOG CABIN SONG BOOK

## OF 1840.

Revised for the Campaign of 1888, with numerous New Songs to
Patriotic Airs.

EDITED BY

O. C. HOOPER.

COLUMBUS, O.:
A. H. SMYTHE,
1888.

# PREFACE.

[ Reprinted from the Edition of 1840.]

Who can not enjoy a good song? Who can not join in one with heart and voice in joyful response? The enthusiasm of a happy people always did and always will break forth in song. A song is the language of a cheerful heart, the overflowing of a buoyant impulse. Nothing ever exceeded the rapidity with which, in these times of feeling and patriotic action, the merry Harrisonian Log Cabin Songs have rushed through the country. Everybody is singing them, and everybody but the sour and crabbed Locofocos is delighted with their simplicity and spirit. It is to meet the wants of the Harrison boys, to furnish them all with a supply of these patriotic and pithy songs, that this little work is compiled. We trust that every free-hearted son of the West will furnish himself with a copy, that he may be prepared to while away the hours of labor and domestic recreation with a cheerful song of Liberty and lift up his voice in chorus with the whole united nation in a chorus of triumph over the downfall of corruption and tyranny.

It is needless to add much, if anything, to the foregoing sentences, written in the blaze of political enthusiasm nearly half a century ago, so forcibly and well do they express the sentiments of the publisher of this later volume. The nomination of a younger Tippecanoe to the high office of President under circumstances not unsimilar to those existing in 1840, has suggested a revision of the old songs that stirred the hearts of our fathers and grandfathers. A few of the songs have been taken verbatim from the old songster; the majority of them, however, have been remodeled and adapted in their wording to the occasion. Still other new songs have been written for the book and some have been appropriated with proper credit to the author or publication.

A significant fact is the large number of songs that have been written since the nomination of Harrison and Morton, and been adapted to popular and patriotic airs. It means that the spring of enthusiasm has been touched in an exceptionally strong manner. This will, doubtless, be a singing campaign; and, if one-half the pleasure is derived from this young Tippecanoe song book that was derived from its predecessor, the object of its publication will have been fully attained.

## TIPPECANOE SONG.

AIR--"*Rosin the Bow.*"

The voice of the nation has spoken,
  The Democrats shake in their shoes;
The sceptre of Grover is broken;
  He shrinks at the glorious news.

CHORUS.

All hail to the glorious West!
  Log cabins and yeomen, to you!
The land of the brave and the blest,
  The home of old Tippecanoe!

G. Cleveland, these four years has mocked us,
  His flesh is no sign of reform;
With promises false he has stocked us,
  And now he must go with the storm.

CHORUS.—All hail, etc.

Our shops he would like to demolish
  With blows of the bludgeon "Free Trade."
And so in November we'll polish
  This Grover with Harrison's aid!

CHORUS.—All hail, etc.

Hail East, and the North, South and West,
  The spirit of '40 renew;
Choose, yeomen, the man who is best—
  The grandson of Tippecanoe.

# LOG CABIN AND HARD CIDER.

AIR—"*Auld Lang Syne.*"

Should good old cider be despised
  And ne'er regarded more?
Should plain log cabins be despised
  Our fathers built of yore?
For the true old style, my boys!
  For the true old style!
Let's take a mug of cider now
  For the true old style!

We've tried experiments enough
  Of fashions new and vain,
And now we mean to settle down
  To good old times again.
For the good old ways, my boys!
  For the good old ways!
Let's take a mug of cider now
  For the good old ways.

We've had four years of Grover C.,
  And that has been enough,
And yet they want to put him back
  In company with Snuff.
But Tip's grandson, my boys,
  But Tip's grandson,
They'll find has been elected when
  November's voting 's done!

Then give us your good hands, my boys!
  And here's a hand for you!
We'll quaff the good old cider yet
  To old Tippecanoe!
To old Tippecanoe, my boys!
  To old Tippecanoe,
For Ben will give another life
  To old Tippecanoe!

And surely you will give your vote
  And surely I will, too;
And we'll clear the way to Washington
  For young Tippecanoe!
For Tip-pe-ca-noe, my boys!
  For Tip-pe-ca-noe!
We'll take a mug of cider yet
  For Tip-pe-ca-noe.

----

## GENERAL HARRISON.
### Air—"*Pizen Sarpient.*"

When British foemen swarmed around
And burned our cabins to the ground,
                    Ri tu ral, etc.,
A gallant boy, brave Harrison,
By noble deeds bright laurels won,
                    Ri tu ral, etc.,
He fought by Wayne, where brave men bled,
And where the ground was strewn with dead,
                    Ri tu ral, etc.,

And where the battle fiercest seemed,
His ready blade in combat gleamed,
                        Ri tu ral, etc.,
He spent long years in hardy fight,
And always kept his laurels bright,
                        Ri tu ral, etc.,
And at the end the people bent
Their wills and made him President,
                        Ri tu ral, etc.


When British foemen swarmed again
To pauperize our workingmen, Ri tu ral, etc.,
Another Harrison appeared
To save the weal Protection reared,
                        Ri tu ral, etc.,
With flashing eye and earnest word
He fought where Free Trade foes were heard,
                        Ri tu ral, etc.,
And bore off honors bravely won,
This other, later Harrison, Ri tu ral, etc.,
And now when traitors here begot
Would give our mills to rust and rot,
                        Ri tu ral, etc.,
He leads the van with flashing blade,
And calls all patriots to his aid, Ri tu ral, etc.,
We'll rise and treachery resent,
And make our Ben the President,
                        Ri tu ral, etc.

# WHAT HAS CAUSED THIS GREAT COM-MOTION?

AIR—"*Little Pig's Tail.*"

Oh, what has caused this great commotion,
Motion, motion, our country through?
    It is the ball
    A-rolling on
  For Tippecanoe and Morton, too,
  For Tippecanoe and Morton, too!
And with them we'll beat Stephen Grove,
Grove, Grove is a used-up "cove,"
And with them we'll beat Stephen Grove!

Just as they did in eighteen-forty,
Forty, forty, the country through,
    We'll raise this year
    A rousing cheer
  For Tippecanoe and Morton, too,
  For Tippecanoe and Morton, too!
And with them we'll beat Stephen Grove,
Grove, Grove is a used-up "cove,"
And with them we'll beat Stephen Grove!

Our fight is this year for protection,
Tection, tection the country through!
    We'll fill, ourselves,
    The merchants' shelves
  With Tippecanoe and Morton, too,
  With Tippecanoe and Morton, too!
And with them we'll beat Stephen Grove,

Grove, Grove is a used-up "cove,"
And with them we'll beat Stephen Grove!

The toilers in our mills and factories,
Factories, factories, the country through
    Will have good pay
    For every day,
  With Tippecanoe and Morton, too,
  With Tippecanoe and Morton, too!
And with them we'll beat Stephen Grove,
Grove, Grove is a used-up "cove,"
And with them we'll beat Stephen Grove!

The men who farm and shear the fleeces,
Fleeces, fleeces, the country through
    Will leave their wool
    To take a pull
  For Tippecanoe and Morton, too,
  For Tippecanoe and Morton, too!
And with them we'll beat Stephen Grove,
Grove, Grove is a used-up "cove,"
And with them we'll beat Stephen Grove!

The honest miners who are digging,
Digging, digging, the country through,
    Need not compete
    With slaves for meat,
  With Tippecanoe and Morton, too,
  With Tippecanoe and Morton, too!
And with them we'll beat Stephen Grove,
Grove, Grove is a used-up "cove,"
And with them we'll beat Stephen Grove!

The boys in blue who fought in sixty,
Sixty, sixty, the country through,
    Will fight again
    With gallant Ben,
  Young Tippecanoe and Morton, too,
  Young Tippecanoe and Morton, too!
And with them we'll beat Stephen Grove,
Grove, Grove, is a used-up "cove,"
And with them we'll beat Stephen Grove!

The Demmies, Englishmen and Mugwumps,
Mugwumps, Mugwumps, the country through,
    May all unite,
    And yet we'll fight
  For Tippecanoe and Morton, too,
  For Tippecanoe and Morton, too!
And with them we'll beat Stephen Grove,
Grove, Grove is a used-up "cove,"
And with them we'll beat Stephen Grove!

## YOUNG TIP'S BROOM.
### Air—"*Buy a Broom.*"

ome, patriots, come, and let's clear out the kitchen,
  Let's sweep out the parlor and clean the east room,
rive the Reformer whose fingers are itching
  To strangle our trade—so take a new broom!
    Take a broom, young Tip's broom?
    Come, every Republican, handle a broom!
o put out this Grover, who long has annoyed us,
  And all his associate lords of misrule,

Will be the best business that ever employed us
　Since helping to put the school dunce on his stool.
　　Take a broom, young Tip's broom?
　　Come, Randall, and handle our youthful Tip's broom

We've high tariff duties, let's dare to maintain them
　In spite of this Grover, Carlisle and them all;
The signs they can't read, so let Daniel explain them—
　Interpret the writing that's writ on the wall.
　　Take a broom, young Tip's broom?
　　Come, all ye Protectionists, handle a broom!

When the contest shall come, let us all do our duty,
　And make a clean sweep of our thirty-eight rooms;
We'll send the Experiment's crew and their booty
　To South Seas exploring with lots of old brooms.
　　Take a broom, young Tip's broom?
　　Come, patriot sweepers, and use a new broom!

Reform the Reformers and sweep out corruption!
　Let tyrants and spoilsmen, with faces of gloom
Hear　the　rumbling　and　throes　of　the　earthquake's
　　　eruption,
　The voice of the nation deciding their doom.
　　Take a broom, young Tip's broom?
　　To sweep out corruption—come, take a new broom.

To end all this warring, defaulting and scheming,
　This war upon labor, and credit, and banks,
On commerce and trading a new light is gleaming;
　The people will soon put an end to their pranks
　　With a broom, young Tip's broom,
　　They'll drive out the spoilers by using Tip's broom.

13

## LOG CABIN SONG.

AIR—"*Highland Laddie.*"

Oh, where, tell me where, was your Buckeye Cabin
    made?
Oh, where, tell me where, was your Buckeye Cabin
    made?
'Twas built among the merry boys who plied the plow
    and spade,
Where the Log Cabin stood in the bonnie Buckeye
    shade.
      CHORUS —'Twas built, etc.

Oh, what, tell me what, was that Buckeye Cabin's fate?
Oh, what, tell me what, was that Buckeye Cabin's fate?
We wheeled it to the Capital, and placed it there elate,
As a token and a sign of the bonnie Buckeye State.

      CHORUS—We wheeled it, etc.

Oh, why, tell me why, did your Buckeye Cabin go?
Oh, why, tell me why, did your Buckeye Cabin go?
It went against the spoilsmen — for well its builders
    knew,
It was Harrison that fought for the Cabins long and true.

      CHORUS — It went against, etc.

And how, tell me how, can that Cabin live again?
And how, tell me how, can that Cabin live again?
It can live in the memory of brave and loyal men;
It can live in the battle for our gallant leader, Ben.

CHORUS — It can live, etc.

Oh, what, tell me what, does this Cabin represent?
Oh, what, tell me what, does this Cabin represent?
It represents the homes where the Free Trade robber
　　went,
And sought to take a dollar and to leave a paltry cent.

CHORUS — It represents, etc.

By whom, tell me whom, will the battle next be won?
By whom, tell me whom, will the battle next be won?
The winner will be Harrison, for we are quite too wise
To starve, that foreigners may eat and grow to Cleve-
　　land's size.

CHORUS —The winner, etc.

Oh, what, tell me what, will Grover Cleveland do?
Oh, what, tell me what, will Grover Cleveland do?
He'll travel back to New York State, a-looking awful
　　blue,
While the Log Cabins ring with "Young Tippecanoe!"
　　CHORUS — He'll travel, etc.

---

## THE ROUGH LOG CABIN.

AIR—*"Rambling Wreck."*

I love the rough log cabin,
　　It tells of olden time
When a hardy and an honest class
　　Of freemen in their prime,

First left their father's peaceful home
  Where all was joy and rest,
With their axes on their shoulders
  And sallied for the West.

Of logs they built a sturdy pile,
  With slabs they roofed it o'er;
With wooden latch and hinges rude,
  They hung the clumsy door,
And for the little window lights
  In size of two feet by two,
They used such sash as could be got
  In regions that were new.

The chimney was composed of slats
  Well interlaid with clay,
And stood a sight we seldom see
  In this a later day;
And there on stones for fire-dogs
  A rousing fire was made,
While round it sat a hardy crew
  With none to make afraid.

I love the old Log Cabin,
  For there in early days
Long lived the honest Harrison,
  Of rough but noble ways,
The people made him President,
  And they will do the same
This year with him who justly shares
  His grandsire's name and fame.

# THE HERO STATESMAN.

AIR—"*The Campbells are Coming.*"

He comes from the West in the strength of his name,
The favored of song and a hero in fame;
He's the people's own choice and his resting shall be
At the side of the brave in the hearts of the free;
No more in the shade of retirement he's laid
Where the warrior's plume rests with his chivalrous
      blade,
For his country demands his true service again,
To protect with his sword and defend with his pen.

CHORUS.

He comes from the West in the strength of his name,
The favored of song and a hero in fame;
He's the people's own choice and his resting shall be
At the side of the brave, in the hearts of the free.

When joined with the wise and engaged with the great
To act for his country in councils of state,
No traitor unscathed shall escape from his hand—
The boldest he'll sweep from a place in the land.
Though dastards revile and though cowards defame
They dim not the glory of Harrison's name;
And louder and louder our plaudits shall rise
For the hero so brave and the statesman so wise.

CHORUS—He comes from the West, etc.

# REPORT

### OF THE COMMITTEE APPOINTED BY THE PEOPLE TO INVITE MR. CLEVELAND INTO A "STATE OF RETIRACY." •

DIRGE —"*Burial of Sir John Moore.*"

Not a sigh was heard, not a farewell groan,
　Though he looked confoundedly flurried;
No patriot's breast was heard to moan,
　As from the White House he was hurried;
He streaked it out darkly at dead of night,
　The way with his grapplers feeling,
And he seemed by the Pan-Electric light
　Like a rogue just caught at sheep stealing.

No useless corset encircled his breast,
　Nor in ruffles nor jewels we found him;
Yet he looked like a chap that had feathered his nest
　With the people's earnings around him.
Long and loud were the curses said,
　And spoke more in anger than sorrow,
As Grover was out from the White House led
　And thrown on the cruel to-morrow.

Startled and wild was his cat-like tread,
　As he crawled on, weak as a pillow;
Like a hyena scared from the feast of the dead,
　As the red morning breaks o'er the billow.
Lightly they'll talk of this man who is gone;
　O'er promises broken upbraid him;
But little we'll reck, so they let him sneak on,
　To the grave where the willows will shade him.

But half of our grateful task was done,
   When the clock tolled the hour so desiring;
And we knew by the boom of a Harrison gun
   That the rest of the crew were retiring.
Down slowly and sadly the Bourbons came
   To the street from the uppermost story;
In a rail-fence fashion they reeled on home,
   And left Tip alone in his glory.

---

## LET FAME PUT HER TRUMP.

Let fame put her trump to the lip of the morn
   And rouse up the slumbering day;
On the wings of the wind be the blast onward borne
   Till it dies in the ether away.
But on the broad hills let it lay
   And echo the green valley o'er,
That a chieftain exists who, if given full sway,
   Shall this country's lost lustre restore.

From the north to the south, from the east to the west,
   From the center all round to the sea,
On the pinions of time that are never at rest,
   It is borne to the tyrants that be.
Then tremble, ye Bourbons, and flee
   For the moments of reckoning come,
More appalling than tempests that scourge the dark sea,
   Or the war-notes of tempest and drum.

From the long dreary night of misrule and dismay
  A whole people awake to the light,
While the dark clouds of error are breaking away,
  And the morning of truth dawning bright;
Again in her splendor and might,
  Fair Freedom unveils to the view,
And points to the chief whose integrity's flight
  Shall the stars of her glory renew.

Betrayed by false statements, the sons of the soil
  Long in error and darkness did grope,
While the vampires bore off the reward of their toil,
  And withered each promise of hope;
But a chieftain there is who shall cope
  With the spoilers with Hercules' arm,
While the phalanx of freemen, unscathed and unbroke,
  The abuses of power shall disarm.

He was tried in the battle and ne'er known to yield,
  Lang syne in the days of our pride;
A sage in the Senate, a chief in the field,
  On whom sages and warriors relied;
They will rally again at his side
  As they did when the hot bullets flew,
And he'll lead them to conquest and glory beside,
  This grandson of Tippecanoe.

At the sound of the blast cheering onward amain,
  Prosperity lifts her pale head
And looks, as her eye brightens up once again,

Like a vestal escaped from the dead;
Toward our chieftain her arms are outspread,
　Who her beauty and strength shall restore,
And robe her anew in the white, blue and red
　That so gracefully veiled her before.

Then pour a libation, and bear it on high
　And let Fame give the word of command,
While the eagle of victory stoops from the sky
　And hovers above the green land.
Round the altar of Freedom we stand
　With the swords of our country in view,
And accoutred for battle, pledge heart and pledge hand
　To the grandson of Tippecanoe.

---

## THE FLAG WILL LEAD.

The spoilsmen are fretful and gloomy as night,
　Their " Denmark is rotten " about;
The party's perplexed and in horrible plight,
　For Grover, they know, must go out.
　　Our flag, like the sign to the Roman, I ween,
　　　Will lead us to glory—and who
　　Wouldn't stick to that flag while a star's to be seen,
　　　The flag of old Tippecanoe?

The sceptre of power from Judah must go;
　The game of Sir Grover is played;
The people insist on Protection, you know,
　Denouncing his scheme of Free Trade.

Then on to the rescue, my hearties, we move,
  Protection will stand, if we do;
Let's follow our leader, and royally prove
  Our love for young Tippecanoe!

Our ship Constitution, though staunch in her hull,
  Has been pitching hard in the storm,
But safely we'll moor her, so on the ropes pull;
  Steer straight for the haven Reform!
    But the ship, to be saved, a new master must have,
      With a new set of tars for her crew;
    From the State of New York her lieutenant must
      come,
    Her captain from Tippecanoe!

When war's deadly summons had led us to blows,
  Where was tenderfoot Grover then found?
In the rear of all dangers, lamenting his woes;
  He hated the battle's dread sound.
    Where was Harrison then? On the field of his fame!
      There proved himself gallant and true;
    The roar of the cannon was music to him —
    The grandson of Tippecanoe!

When peace, after victories, came to the land,
  Back home, with proud laurels, he came,
And now, at a patriot people's demand,
  He'll march to the apex of fame.
    Our flag, like the sign to the Roman, I ween,
      Will lead us to victory—for who
    Wouldn't follow the flag while a star's to be seen,
      Or a rag of the red, white and blue?

# YE JOLLY YOUNG LADS.

AIR—*"Rosin the Bow."*

Ye jolly young lads of the nation
  And all ye sick Democrats, too,
Come out from the Free Trader party
  And vote for young Tippecanoe.

CHORUS—And vote for young Tippecanoe, etc.

The ides of November is coming,
  The Demmies begin to look blue;
They know there's no chance for poor Grover
  For we'll elect Tippecanoe.

CHORUS—For we'll elect Tippecanoe, etc.

Good men from the Demmies are flying
  Which makes them look kinder askew,
For they see that the numbers are swelling
  That follow young Tippecanoe.

CHORUS—That follow young Tippecanoe, etc.

His grandfather lived in a cabin,
  And drank mugs of good cider, too,
But he got to be President, certain,
  And so will young Tippecanoe.

CHORUS—And so will young Tippecanoe, etc.

Our slogan of battle, " Protection !"
  Our flag, the old red, white and blue!

We'll march to a glorious triumph
  This year, with young Tippecanoe.

CHORUS—This year, with young Tippecanoe, etc.


And if on the march we get thirsty,
  I'll tell you just what we will do—
We'll carry a keg of hard cider
  And drink with young Tippecanoe.
CHORUS—And drink with young Tippecanoe, etc.

---

## NEW COMIC SONG.

AIR —"*Hey, Come Along, Josey.*"

Come listen to me, and I'll sing you a song,
Which, I promise you, shall not be long;
And I know you'll say it's a first-rate thing,
And dis is de tune dat I will sing:
      Hey, cum along, jim along, Josey.
      Hey, cum along, jim along, Jo.

De Republicans, you know, next fall
Is goin' ter stop de Bourbon ball;
Ginrawl Harrison is too strong for Grover,
And at the lexshun will turn him over.
      Hey, cum along, jim along, Josey.
      Hey, cum along, jim along, Jo.

De Demmies say dey will no hab him,
Kase how he born in a log cabin;
But de peeple say dey do not kere,

He shall hab de White House 'fore a year.
    Hey, cum along, jim along, Josey.
    Hey, cum along, jim along, Jo.

Dey say his gran'pa drank hard cider,
But dey only spread his fame de wider,
And dey may ober dere shampane,
Make fun ob him, but it's all in vain.
    Hey, cum along, jim along, Josey.
    Hey, cum along, jim along, Jo.

Yes, let um laf at his old granny,
But how he walloped little Vanny!.
He put de Locos on de run,
And den he entered Washington.
    Hey, cum along, jim along, Josey,
    Hey, cum along, jim along, Jo.

And dat's de way young Tippecanoe
Will with this Free Trade Grover do.
An' Grove and all will make dere tracks
As if the debbil war at dere backs.
    Hey, cum along, jim along, Josey.
    Hey, cum along, jim along, Jo.

An' now, gentle folks, I bid you good bye,
Don't let de Demmies frow chalk in yer eye.
And when to de city de Ginrawl you bring,
Dis nigger'll be dere all ready to sing.
    Hey, cum along, jim along, Josey.
    Hey, cum along, jim along, Jo.

# SHOULD BRAVE SOLDIERS BE FORGOT?

AIR —*"Auld Lang Syne."*

Should brave old soldiers be forgot?
  Should patriots fail to twine
Wreaths, glorious wreaths, for those who fought
  In the days of old lang syne?
No!  Long as life endures will we
  Deep in our hearts enshrine
The names of those who made us free
  In the days of old lang syne.

Proud England, gloating o'er her Crown,
  And King and Right's Divine,
Sent forth her slaves to chain us down
  In the days of old lang syne;
But Freedom's champions averred
  They'd make the Lion whine,
And nobly did they keep their word
  In the days of old lang syne.

They drew a charter, strong and full;
  Nor did they fear to sign
The bulletin that pricked John Bull,
  And cut in every line.
Among the hearts of flint, whose fire
  Lit up the flame benign,
Was Harrison — Tip's great-grandsire —
  A Whig of old lang syne.

But not the grandsire's fame alone
  Exalts our Harrison;
He has bright laurels of his own,
  In hard fought battles won;
For when rebellion raised its head
  He led a royal line,
Fought treason till he left it dead,
  In days of old lang syne.


And what was Cleveland?   Where or when
  Did he lead on the brave,
Or raise his voice or wield his pen,
  Or ope his purse to save?
Oh, yes; according to repute
  Did Grover Cleveland shine,
By sending out a substitute
  In war days, old lang syne.


And Thurman, he who stands beside
  This Grover, what did he?
Did he rush where the crimson tide
  Flowed fast to make men free?
He stayed at home and styled the war
  Disastrous and malign,
And not a flag or musket bore,
  In days of old lang syne.


The knapsack pillowed Harry's head,
  The hard ground eased his toils;
While Cleveland slept on downy bed,

And Thurman nursed his boils.
Shall these men then exalted be?
  Shall loyalty decline?
Forbid it Heaven!　Forbid it, ye
  Who bled in old lang syne!

Let those who love the Free Trade charms,
  Hard work and little pay,
Closed working-shops and mortgaged farms,
  Extol King Grover's sway;
But we have solemnly affirmed
"No Free Trade, sir, in mine!"
And Grover shan't be second-termed,
  Not by an old lang syne!

---

## BUCKEYE BOYS.

AIR—"*Swiss Boy.*"

Come arouse ye, arouse ye, my brave Buckeye boys!
  Take the ax and to labor away!
The sun is up with ruddy beam
The Buckeye blooms beside the stream;
    Come, arouse ye, etc.

Love ye not, love ye not, O my brave Buckeye boys
  To rally with Tippecanoe?
For the hero, patriot, brave and free
Waits to assert your liberty!
    Love ye not, etc.

To the polls, to the polls then my brave Buckeye boys,
    To the rescue then haste ye away.
The cup we fill, the hard cider pass
In friendship around until the last;
With a shout, with a shout, go the brave Buckeye boys
    With young Tip to the White House away.

---

### ON TO VICTORY!
AIR—"*Scots wha hae.*"

Men, whose sires for freedom bled!
Men, whom patriots oft have led!
Men, by treasury spoils unfed,
    On, to victory!

Now's the day and now's the hour!
See approach the tyrant's power!
Shall we to the tyrant's cower?
    Shall we turn and flee?

Hear the foe's insulting cry!
Hear them boast of victory nigh!
Men, that boasting we defy—
    We shall still be free!

What care we if Mugwumps yield?
Here's our chosen battle-field,
Grasp the sword and brace the shield!
    On, to victory!

Rally men in Labor's cause!
Fight for honest Tariff laws!
Falter not, nor turn, nor pause!
    On, to victory!

'Tis a Harrison leads on!
He's a gallant Buckeye son!
Think of former triumphs won!
On, to victory!

---

## THE OLD BATTLE FLAG.

AIR—"*Marching Through Georgia.*"

Hoist the good old flag, my boys, we always loved
  so well,
And fling it to the breeze again, 'though torn by shot
  and shell,
And as we gaze upon its stars we'll think of those
  who fell,
  While we were fighting in Dixie.

CHORUS.

Hurrah! Hurrah! we bring the jubilee,
Hurrah! Hurrah! for the flag that made you free;
So we sang the chorus on the land and on the sea,
  While we were fighting in Dixie.

How the boys shouted when they saw the old flag wave
In the thickest of the fight, where none dare go but
  brave,
And many a comrade lost his life and found a soldier's
  grave,
  While we were fighting in Dixie.
    CHORUS—Hurrah! Hurrah! etc.

Yes, and there are soldier boys who weep with honest tears
When they see that tattered flag they followed for four years,
And every time it's raised aloft we'll greet it with three cheers,
'Though we are marching through Dixie.

CHORUS — Hurrah! Hurrah! etc.

Then rally round the flag again—the emblem of the free,
It is the starry banner, boys, that floats o'er you and me,
The same we followed through the fight, wherever it might be,
While we were fighting in Dixie.

CHORUS — Hurrah! Hurrah! etc.

Then let us once again, old boys, our solemn vows renew,
To stand by that starry flag, the red, white and blue,
And never shall they be forgot, our comrades brave and true,
Who died while fighting in Dixie.

CHORUS — Hurrah! Hurrah! etc.

—*Jerry Elbert, First Virginia*

## CAMPAIGN SONG.

AIR —"*Good-by, My Lover, Good-by.*"

O Democrats, hear the trumpet blow,
Good-by, free traders, good-by!

Pack up your grips, its time to go,
  Good-by, free traders, good-by!
Protection is the people's wealth,
  Good-by, free traders, good-by!
And we will guard the Nation's health,
  Good-by, free traders, good-by!

CHORUS.

  By, Cleveland, by, O!
  By, Thurman, by, O!
  Home and prosperity!
  Old British free traders, good-by!

The flag is floating in the breeze,
  Good-by, bandanna, Good-by!
The stars and stripes will better please,
  Good-by, bandanna, good-by!
We'll nail our banner to the mast,
  Good-by, bandanna, good-by!
Your old red rag won't stand the blast,
  Good-by, bandanna, good-by!

CHORUS.

  By, Cleveland, by, O!
  By, Thurman, by, O!
  Wave, flag of loyalty!
  Old red bandanna, good-by!

Old Indiana names the man,
  Good-by, dear Grover, good-by!
Come here and beat him if you can,

Good-by, dear Grover, good-by!
Ben Harrison is the man to win,
  Good-by, dear Grover, good by!
Go home and watch our BEN-JAM-IN!
  Good-by, big Grover, good-by!

CHORUS.

  By, Cleveland, by, O!
  By, Thurman, by, O!
  Harrison and victory!
  Four hundred pounder, good-by!

They brought poor Thurman out too late,
  Good-by, Old Roman, good-by!
In Morton he will meet his fate,
  Good-by, Old Roman, good-by!
Our soldier Ben the land will sweep,
  Good-by, Old Roman, good-by!
November leaves shall bury you deep!
  Good-by, Old Roman, good-by!

CHORUS.

  By, Cleveland, by, O!
  By, Thurman, by, O!
  Union and purity!
  Old foul bandanna, good-by!
                    — *Richard Lew Dawson.*

## THE PEOPLE'S SONG.

AIR—" *Gilderoy*."

We long to see the season come
When we can vote for Harrison,
For there is nothing can prevent
His being the next President;
He leads the cause against Free Trade,
And we propose to give him aid;
O, Grover dear, you'd better run
Than measure swords with Harrison!

When some were in their cradles rock'd,
Their fathers round the Hero flock'd.
The fight was hard, but still they won,
Led on by General Harrison;
But now with double force they come,
The war-worn soldier, with his son,
They strike the time without the drum,
Both right and left, for Harrison.

Supporting General Harrison,
The people have no risk to run —
For he can first adjust their laws,
Then with his sword maintain their cause.
Then raise the banner till it floats,
While men are handing in their votes;
And may their ballots tell as one,
Success to General Harrison.

Then let this song, for one, be sung,
As clear as rebel rifles rung,

By middle-aged, old and young,
Without one jar or faltering tongue;
And let the spangled banner wave,
High on the breeze, above the brave,
While they proclaim the work is done,
We'll join for General Harrison.

# Later Songs.

## THE COLLAR AND THE KERCHIEF.
### AIR—"*John Brown.*"

Grover Cleveland is a collar of extraordinary size,
So that many men mistake him for a corset in disguise,
He standeth on his tip-toes and he looketh with surprise,
    As we go marching on.

        CHORUS.—Glory, etc.


When first he was invented for the Democratic shirt,
He was laundried by a mugwump who declared him
        free from dirt;
In spite of that, he's got to go, we might just here
        insert,
        As we go marching on.

        CHORUS—Glory, etc.


The Muggies put about him for to keep him clean and
    warm,

A tie of beauteous colors that was called by them "Reform,"
But that was blown to glory in the office-seeking storm,
    As we go marching on.

        CHORUS—Glory, etc.

Now the Democrats into his mammoth button-hole
    have tied
A dullish red Bandana that is very long and wide,
And have hung the two above them to excite the party
    pride
    As we go marching on.

        CHORUS—Glory, etc.

Against their mammoth collar, and their kerchief, too,
    of red,
We'll hoist the starry banner at our mighty column's
    head
And never halt till Harrison to Washington we've led,
    As we go marching on.

        CHORUS—Glory, etc.

                —*O. C. Hooper.*

---

## PEACH TREE CREEK.

At Peachtree creek in Sixty-four,
    Hood's rebels held the summit:
Their lines were long and full and strong,
    And straight as line and plummet.

Below them stood the Union ranks,
   And waved the starry banner,
And at the front Ben Harrison
   With his Seventieth Indiana.

"Charge at them, men!" cried sturdy Ben;
   "What, colonel, without orders?"
"Yes, charge the hill! and with a will
   We'll sweep the rebel borders."

And in the van, that gallant man,
   Ben Harrison, led the onset,
And drove out Hood and all his brood
   And held the hill at sunset.

"Bravissimo!" cried fighting Joe,
   "Ben Harrison's no Quaker;
I'll make him here a brigadier
   For Peachtree and Resaca."

Now once again the Union men,
   Demanding home protection,
Place in the van that gallant man,
   And promise him election.

"Charge up the hill!" again he shouts,
   "Down with the red bandanna!"
Up, boys, and vote!  Again promote
   Brave Ben of Indiana!
              —*Boston Traveller.*

## THE RACERS.

AIR—"*Yankee Doodle.*"

Hurrah! Hurrah for Harrison!
  Hurrah for Levi Morton!
The nags are picked the race to run,
  Oh, don't you hear them snortin'?

CHORUS:

Hurrah, then, for the bonny flag!
  It beats the old Bandana!
We'll carry with it New York State,
  And also Indiana!

The "off" one there's from New York State,
  The "nigh" from Indiana;
The "off" will run 'gainst Grover great,
  The "nigh" against Bandana.

Now Levi has a pedigree
  And Ben is no beginner;
His grandsire in the Derby ran
  Of '40 and was winner.

For Harrison and Morton cheer!
  They're good old stock, remember;
Their powers of staying will appear
  On homestretch in November.

If Levi wins in New York State
  And Ben in Indiana,
'Twill mean "Get out" for Grover great
  And "Keep out" for Bandana.

*—Columbus Dispatch.*

## READY FOR THE BATTLE.

AIR- *Policemen's Chorus—Pirates of Penzance—"When a Felon's not
Engaged."*

We are ready for the battle of November
That shall settle Grover Cleveland's little fate,
And we feel no whit of fear, for we remember
We have got a soldier-statesman candidate!
We have drawn our swords to fight for trade protection,
And we follow gallant General Harrison!
Be happy now, dear Grover, the election
Will make your lot a most unhappy one!
        We will follow gallant General Harrison,
        Making Grover's lot a most unhappy one.

We've unfurled the starry banner of the nation;
The nation is our promise and our care;
The flag floats on, while hills' reverberation
Proclaims the people's joy to see it there,
For industries must not be unprotected,
And we who do not want our trade undone
This autumn, mean to see with vim elected
A gentleman whose name is Harrison.
        And we who do not want that trade undone
        Will vote this fall for General Harrison.

We will march unto the voting place, this autumn,
    With a straight Protection ballot and a spade;
We'll teach the Demmies there when we have caught 'em
    And we'll dig a grave and there inter Free Trade.
We'll bury it so deep no trumpet sounded,
    And no English-manufactured army gun

They may fire above the grave that we have rounded,
  Can awake the Star-Eyed Goddess's dead son.
    And no English-manufactured army gun
    Shall awake the Star-Eyed Goddess's dead son!

Grover Cleveland is a John Bull in appearance;
  They are brothers in the roundness of the vest,
They are brothers in denouncing interference
  With the business of that land both love the best.
Then there's Thurman, who is also very foreign —
  A gentleman is he from ancient Rome;
And he doesn't seem to care a yellow florin
  For the industries we've nurtured here at home.
    Neither Cleveland nor this gentleman from Rome
    Care for industries we've nurtured here at home!

But there's Harrison and Morton for Protection!
  And so we say we're ready for the fight!
We are bound to win this National election,
  For America, Protection and the Right!
No friend of Johnny Bull shall longer rule us,
  Not even if he weighed a half a ton;
And no gentleman from ancient Rome shall fool us,
  For we're going to vote for Benny Harrison!
    If Grover Cleveland weighed a half a ton,
    We still should vote for Benny Harrison!
                                        — *O. C. Hooper.*

## THE TWO ENSIGNS.

In '76 a patriot band —
  The brave, the tried and true—

Unfurled our standard to the breeze:
The dear red, white and blue.

In '61, o'er loyal hosts,
Our ensign kissed the breeze,
While the "old bandanna" stifled
Thurman's Hyperborean sneeze.

In '64, 'midst battle smoke,
Our flag of all the free
Waved proudly o'er brave Harrison,
With Sherman, to the sea.

In '87, when Cleveland said
The rebel flags should go,
Old Allen G. unfurled his rag
And calmly took a blow.

One is the emblem of free trade
And rampant anarchy;
The other floats throughout the land,
The ensign of the free.

And when you know the use of each
The contrast wider grows;
One fires the patriotic heart —
The other wipes the nose.

—*C. E. Blossom*

Miamisburg, O.

## THE RED, WHITE AND BLUE.

TUNE—*"Red, White and Blue."*

Democrats may flourish their bandannas—
　The flag of our country we'll wave.
The "boys" from the lakes to savannas
　Once more this grand Union will save.
With Harrison and Morton for leaders,
　We'll sweep victoriously through;
From Maine to shores the of Pacific,
　And carry the red, white and blue.

### CHORUS.

And carry the red, white and blue.
And carry the red, white and blue.
　From Maine to the shores of Pacific
We'll carry the red, white and blue.

'Mid the shrieks of the shells and the bullets,
　Where carnage and death held high glee,
And patriots were falling the thickest,
　Where agony only you'd see,
There thousands and thousands perished,
　To their country and Union true,
For love of the flag that they cherished,
　For love of the red, white and blue!

### CHORUS.

O, prate not of Cleveland's reforming,
　Or Thurman's great love for the "boys;"
When Democrats the North were a storming,
　It made the "Old Roman" rejoice.

42

Let Democrats carry bandannas,
  To the flag of the Union we're true,
From the lakes across the savannas
  We'll carry the red, white and blue.

CHORUS.

"Protection to all!" is our slogan,
  No Tories our land shall control,
Led on by the spirit of Logan,
  Protection we'll sound to each Pole!
Let party slaves flourish bandannas,
  To the flag of our Union we're true,
From the lakes across the savannas
  We'll carry the red, white and blue.

CHORUS.

———

## AS HARRISON MARCHES ON.

AIR —"*When Johnnie Comes Marching Home.*"

Come all and sing the jubilee,
  Hurrah! Hurrah!
Harrison is our nominee,
  Hurrah! Hurrah!
With Morton for the second place,
No Democrat can win the race,
And we'll all feel gay
  As Harrison marches on.
                ( Repeat last two lines.)

He is our man to make the fight,
    Hurrah! Hurrah!
Because the people know he's right,
    Hurrah! Hurrah!
With the Stars and Stripes and Ben to lead,
To the White House he will go with speed,
And we'll all feel gay
    As Harrison marches on.
            (Repeat last two lines.)

He's sound upon the tariff plan,
    Hurrah! Hurrah!
He's the friend of every workingman,
    Hurrah! Hurrah!
The business men all know he's great
From Maine unto the Golden Gate;
And we'll all feel gay
    As Harrison marches on.
            (Repeat last two lines.)

Then wave our starry banner high,
    Hurrah! Hurrah!
For Harrison and Morton cry,
    Hurrah! Hurrah!
How the men will cheer and the boys will shout
When the Democrats are all turned out,
And we'll all feel gay
    As Harrison marches on.
            (Repeat last two lines.)
                        — *D. Lace, Chicago.*

# 44

## THE BATTLE CRY, PROTECTION.

Air—"*Battle Cry of Freedom.*"

For America and freedom we take the field again
   Shouting the battle cry, Protection!
And rally round our banner, a host of busy men
   Shouting the battle cry, Protection!

### CHORUS.

America forever!   Hurrah, boys, hurrah!
   Down with the bandanna and up with the stars,
While we rally round the flag, boys, rally once again
   Shouting the battle cry, Protection!

Free trade and English wages we never can endure,
   Shouting the battle cry, Protection!
Our land is for Americans, alike for rich and poor,
   Shouting the battle cry, Protection!

CHORUS—America forever! etc.

For Harrison and Morton we'll rally round the flag,
   Shouting the battle cry, Protection!
And drive the foe before us with their red bandanna rag,
   Shouting the battle cry, Protection!

CHORUS—America, forever! etc.

## OH, GROVER C., MY JO GROVE.

AIR—"*John Anderson, My Jo.*"

Oh, Grover C., my Jo Grove! I wonder what you mean
By such an inconsistent act as that we've lately seen;
You thought a second term, Grove, about four years ago,
A danger to the nation, Oh, Grover C., my Jo.

Oh, Grover C., my Jo Grove, you've climbed the hill of
    state,
And many a cunning trick, man, was fathered in your
    pate;
But now you're tottering down, Grove; how rapidly
    you go!
You'll soon be sprawling at the foot, Oh, Grover C.,
    my Jo!

Oh, Grover C., my Jo Grove, when first we were acquaint
'Tis true you was not slow, Grove, with sinner or with
    saint;
But now you have grown fat, Grove, you never seem to
    know
How fast you're going back again, Oh, Grover C., my Jo.

Oh, Grover C., my Jo Grove, now Thurman is your
    ‹bower,
You've set him up behind you, Grove, to help you ride
    to power,
But he has grown too old, Grove, we all of us well
    know,
To help you much in such a race, Oh, Grover C., my Jo.

Oh, Grover C., my Jo Grove, our faith you did abuse,
And you can't wear again, Grove, the Presidential shoes;
So take yourself away, Grove; clear back to Buffalo,
For Harrison will take your place, Oh, Grover C., my Jo.

---

## THE CATASTROPHE.

AIR.—"*The Bull Dog.*"

Allen Thurman on the bank, Grover Cleveland in the
pool,
Allen Thurman on the bank, Grover Cleveland in the
pool,
Allen Thurman on the bank, Grover Cleveland in the
pool,
"O, help me out and put me on the Presidential stool!"

CHORUS.

Singing tra, la, la, la, la, la, la, singing tra, la, la, la, la,
la, la,
Singing tra, la, la, la, la, la, singing tra, la, la, la, la, la,
Tra, la, la, tra, la, la, tra, la, la, tra, la, la.

Then old Allen stooped to catch him and asked, "What
do I get?"
"O, Allen," answered Grover, "you'll probably get
wet!"

Singing tra, la, la, etc.

"O, Allen, don't forsake him!" the office-holders said;
"Pray what's your fatal soaking to our own loss of
bread?"

Singing tra, la, la, etc.

Then Allen unto Grover threw out a red bandanna,
Which was whirled away to Nowhere on a breeze from
    Indiana.
       Singing tra, la, la, etc.

Allen Thurman on the bank, Grover Cleveland in the
    pool;
While Harrison is sitting on the Presidential stool.
       Singing tra, la, la, etc.

One stuck in Free Trade quicksand and t'other in sur-
    prise
Amused the fickle Goddess who has two stars for eyes.
       Singing tra, la, la, etc.

Said the Goddess, loudly laughing, in manner somewhat
    rude,
"You've carried one State, Grover,— Innocuous Desue-
    tude!"
       Singing tra, la, la, etc.
                    — *O. C. Hooper.*

## THE FREE TRADE BANNER.

AIR—"*When Freedom from Her Mountain Height.*"

When Free Trade, from her topmost crag,
    Unfurled her standard to the air,
She thrust aside the old time flag,
    And set a big bandanna there.
She sprinkled o'er its crimson dyes
The dust that in a snuff-box lies;

She striped its folds, red as a rose,
With snuff that tickles Thurman's nose.       .

When Thurman shall have snuffed and sneezed,
    In "noblest Roman," Ha-kitch-oo,
The Demmies all, with noses greased,
    Will join the sneezing chorus too.
However loud they sneeze and blow,
'Twill be a sound of dismal woe
Compared to that deep-throated cheer
We'll raise for Harrison, this year.

The sound of Allen Thurman's sneeze
    Will pierce the Solid South's ears through.
'Twill go to Britons o'er the seas,
    And they will sneeze by cable, too.
But when the North shall raise her shout,
'Twill drown these foreign sneezers out,
And all the snoozers here at home
Who love this gentleman from Rome!

We love the old Red, White and Blue,
    That Freedom long ago unfurled;
We love our glorious country, too,
    The fairest one in all the world!
We love our mines, we love our mills,
With fervor that our heart-strings thrills.
And we'll prosperity protect,
And see our Harrison elect!

## HARRISON'S THE DANDY.

Cleveland took his hook and line and started off
    a-fishing.
He fished for suckers all the day, but took it out in
    wishing.
It seems the suckers all were off attending decoration,
And this, and other things as bad, raised Grover's indig-
    nation.

### CHORUS.

Yankee Doodle, mind the steps, Ben. Harrison's the
    dandy,
We're sure that in November next we'll vote him in so
    handy.

Says he to Dan, "I'll show 'em how I like this sort of
    fashion.
This waving of the bloody shirt has raised my deepest
    passion.
I'll send for Drum and have them call the Brigadiers
    together;
I'll have them come (I will by gum)! arrayed in hat
    and feather.

"The war is over now, and we should march in one
    procession,
The Southern Democrats in front, the Northern in suc-
    cession.

To prove I mean to treat them white, I'll give them
 back their banners —
The time has come to muster out the pauper Union
 grannies."

"But, noble sire," Dan made reply, "think well before
 you venture.
The times are perilous, and you may meet with public
 censure."
"Well, well, replied the President, "for trouble I'm
 not wishing,
But if the worst comes to the worst, why then I'll go
 a-fishing."

*— Athens Messenger.*

---

## THE FREE-TRADE PINAFORE.

[In Which Captain Cleveland Appears at the Head of the Democratic Crew.]

Capt. Cleveland — I am the captain of the Free Trade
 crew.

Chorus of Democratic Tars — And a right good captain, too.

Capt. C.—You are very, very good, and be it understood,
 I'm in for reform right through.

Chorus —We are very, very good, and be it understood
He's in for reform right through.

Capt. C.— I can trim back and steer with any boss here,
    And I know how to twist and squirm.
I was never known to scorn civil service to reform,
    And I'll never take a second term.

> Chorus—What! never!
> Capt. C.— No, never!
> Chorus.—What! never!
> Capt. C.— Hardly ever!

Chorus — Hardly ever take a second term?
    Then here's one yell and a snicker, too,
    For the one-term captain of the Free Trade crew.
    Then here's one yell and a snicker, too,
    For the captain of the Free Trade crew.

Capt. C.— I've done my best to satisfy you all.

Chorus — And with you we are all content.

Capt. C.—That's an everlasting whopper, but I think it
        only proper
    To return the compliment.

Chorus —That's an everlasting whopper, but he thinks
        it only proper
    To return the compliment.

Capt. C.— I have made a heap of noise, and I've called
        in the boys
    To warm their frozen toes;
I've discouraged all proclivity to partisan activity,
    And I've always worn Free Trade clothes.

Chorus —What! always?
Capt. C.—Yes, always!
Chorus —What! always?
Capt. C.—Well, recently!

Chorus— He's recently donned Free Trade clothes?
Then here's a yell and a snicker, too,
For the free wool captain of the Free Trade crew.
Then here's a yell and a snicker, too,
For the captain of the Free Trade crew.

—*Springfield Union.*

---

## O, GLORIOUS STANDARD!
AIR—"*Hail Columbia.*"

O, glorious standard of the free,
Thou flag of loyal colors three,
    Float ever o'er our hearths and homes,
    Float ever o'er our hearths and homes,
A sign that we our country love,
All foreign lands and suns above,
Float there and, in the breezes swayed,
Proclaim to all who love Free Trade,
At home, abroad, live where they will,
We cling to Trade Protection still!
      Millions to our standard flock,
      Workmen stand like solid rock;
      Free Trade England cannot shake
      Lines that this old flag can make!

Then vote Protection to our mills
And to the land the farmer tills,

For foes are threatening to destroy,
For foes are threatening to destroy;
Let Free Trade hide her dastard head
The land is ours on which we tread;
So rally to the standard on,
For he who leads is Harrison;
Let the battle well be fought,
Glory's best when dearest bought.
    Millions to our standard flock,
    Workmen stand like solid rock;
    Free Trade England cannot shake
    Lines that this old flag can make!

Lo, now a mighty people rise
With cheers exulting rend the skies,
    Brave Harrison in loud huzzas,
    Brave Harrison in loud huzzas,
From east to west the echo rings
And freedom flaps her airy wings,
Rejoiced to see her reign prolonged,
By millions round the hero thronged.
Hoist the banner high in air,
Loyal hearts are everywhere!
    Millions to our standard flock,
    Workmen stand like solid rock;
    Free Trade England cannot shake
    Lines that this old flag can make!

# GWINE TO GIT DAR.

Dar's a-gwine to be a movin' call
  Dis fall at de election,
An' so 'tis bes' dat one and all
  Shall stand up fer protection.
De people am prepared to 'fect
  A clearin' up an sortin';
De leaders dat dey hab selec'
  Am Harrison an' Morton.

CHORUS.

An' dey's gwine to git dar, git dar, git dar,
  Gwine to git dar, sartin;
Gwine to git dar, shore's yer born,
  Wid Harrison an' Morton.

De farmers wid dar clips o' wool,
  De toilers wid dar labor,
Am more dan match for Liverpool
  And British legislator;
Dey overmatch de Cleveland crew,
  An' Thurman's old bandanna;
Dey follers de red, white an' blue,
  Wid Ben of Indiana.

CHORUS.—O, dey's gwine to git dar, etc.

A hero frum de great Norfwes'
  Am jes' de man to lead 'em;
Fer dat de land de fust an' bes'
  Wur consecrate to Freedom.

'Tis foremost in de fight fer man,
  Ob any oder Nation,
An' run upon the slickes' plan
  In all de wide creation.

CHORUS.—O, dey's gwine to git thar, etc.


De cranks may turn an' Mugwumps squirm,
  But "de world do move," for sartin;
An' de order's out for de Cleveland firm,—
  "Git a good ready for departin'."
Millions am a-comin' down wid Blaine,
  An' millions more wid Sherman;
Dis yer am manhood's great campaign
  Fer Yankee, Celt, or German.

CHORUS.—O, dey's gwine to git dar, etc.
                              —*Commercial Gazette.*

---

## GLORIOUS IS OUR CANDIDATE!

AIR—*Policemen's Chorus, Pirates of Penzance* — "*When the Foeman Bares His Steel.*"

  Glorious is our candidate!
  Brave in war and wise in State!
  And we certainly expect
  Him, this autumn, to elect;
  For when foemen would invade
  And the Nation calls for aid,
  Quicker answer comes from none
  Than from gallant Harrison!

Rise, then, lovers of Protection!
Forward, march in this direction!
We must win the next election,
    Or prosperity is gone!
Vote the busy mill preserving!
Vote good pay to those deserving!
Vote against Free Trade, unswerving!
    Vote for gallant Harrison!

Grover Cleveland does his best,
But the greatness of a vest,
And the thoughts by others lent,
Cannot make a President!
He no promises has kept,
At reform he's not adept,
And he serves our foes with zest—
Still, we think, he does his best.

Grover's tried his hand at ruling;
It has been to him a schooling,
But he's daubed us with his drooling,
    And we're very, very tired.
So, to stop his wild cavortin'
And our own distress to shorten,
We're for Harrison and Morton —
    That's a pair to be admired!

Thurman, of the red Bandan,
Goes as Cleveland's second man;
But he cannot do at all
What was planned for him this fall!

Indiana is all right!
And New York is just in sight!
And it's very evident
On Protection they are bent!

Tippecanoe!
And Morton, too!
Then forward on the foe
We go, we go.

—*O. C. Hooper.*

## A SONG OF TWO SOLDIERS.

Air—*"Old Oaken Bucket."*

Oh, dear to my soul are the days of our glory,
The time honored days of our national pride,
When heroes and statesmen ennobled our story,
And boldly the foes of our country defied;
When victory hung o'er our flag proudly waving,
And the battle was fought by the valiant and true,
For our homes and our loved ones the enemy braving,
Oh, then stood the soldier of Tippecanoe.
The iron-armed soldier, the true-hearted soldier,
The gallant old soldier of Tippecanoe.

When dark was the tempest, and hovering o'er us,
The clouds of disunion seemed gathering fast,
Like a ray of bright sunshine he stood out before us,
And the clouds passed away with a hurrying blast.
When the rebel's loud yell and his bayonet flashing,
Spread terror around us and hope was with few,

On then, through the ranks of the enemy dashing,
  Sprang forth to the rescue young Tippecanoe.
    The iron armed soldier, the true hearted soldier,
    The grandson of gallant old Tippecanoe.

When cannons were pealing and brave men were reeling,
  In the cold arms of death from the fire of the foe,
Where balls flew the thickest and blows fell the quickest,
  In the front of the battle bold Harry did go.
The force of the enemy trembled before him,
  And soon from the field of his glory withdrew,
And his warm hearted comrades in triumph cried o'er
    him.
    God bless the brave grandson of Tippecanoe!
    The iron armed soldier, the true hearted soldier,
    The grandson of gallant old Tippecanoe.

And now, since the men have four years held the nation,
  Who trampled our rights in their scorn to the ground,
We will fill their cold hearts with a new trepidation,
  And shout in their ears this most terrible sound —
The people are coming, resistless and fearless,
  To sweep from the White House the reckless old
    crew;
For the woes of the land, since its rulers are tearless,
  We look for relief to young Tippecanoe,
    The iron armed soldier, the true hearted soldier,
    The grandson of gallant old Tippecanoe.

The people are coming from plain and from mountain,
  To join the brave band of the honest and free,

Which grows as the stream from the leaf sheltered
  mountain,
  Spreads broad and more broad tlil it reaches the sea.
No strength can resist it, no force can restrain it,
  What'er may resist, it breaks gallantly through,
And borne by its motion as a ship on the ocean,
  Speeds on in his glory, young Tippecanoe;
    The iron armed soldier, the true hearted soldier,
    The grandson of gallant old Tippecanoe.

---

## THE PRESIDENTIAL FISHERMAN.

Air —"*The Fine Old English Gentleman.*"

Come listen, all ye soldiers who wore the royal blue,
I've got a little story to tell you that is true,
About a "mugwump" President named Cleveland, who
  they say
A year ago a-fishing went on Decoration Day.

So he got his tackle ready, and bait the day before,
Says he, "This Decoration Day's a most confounded
  bore;
What difference does it make to me who wore the blue
  or gray,
Therefore a fisherman I'll be on Decoration Day."

Says he again, "Let others rave and rant about the
  heroes brave,
Who for their country fought and bled, and died the
  land to save.

Why didn't they hire substitutes, so they at home
    could stay,
Like me, and wear their fishing suit on Decoration
    Day?"

So to the Adirondacks with hook and line he went,
And all day long he lunched and fished, this mugwump
    President.
But the loyal fish refused to bite, or with his bait to play,
*They* know that fishing isn't right on Decoration Day.

Then to the White House he returned with disappoint-
    . ment sad,
And told his pretty little wife what sorry luck he'd had.
Says she, "My dear, it served you right; don't go
    again, I pray;
You might have known fish would not bite on Decora-
    tion Day."

Now, let each future President take warning by his fate,
Who, for a second term, like him, would be a candidate,
Just heed this admonition, and do what else you may,
Oh, never go a-fishin' on Decoration day.
                 *—J. L. Boardman, Hillsboro, O.*

---

## WHAT SHALL THE TARIFF BE?

Cutting the tax from the sheep's white wool,
Cutting the tax from the silken spool,
Cutting the tax from the cotton hose,

Cutting the tax from the English clothes;
    What shall the tariff be?
    Oh, what shall the tariff be?

CHORUS.

Cut here by Cleveland and cut there by Mills,
Cut in the platform and cut in bills,
Cut off of everything made here you see,
Free, oh free, shall the tariff be.

Lopping it off from the farmer's flax,
Lopping it off from the cutler's ax;
Lopping it off from the weaver's web,
Lopping it off from the spinner's thread!
    What shall the tariff be?
    Oh, what shall the harvest be?

Paying England for boots and shoes,
Paying England for all that we use,
Starving our labor and shutting our mills,
Killing our commerce with free trade bills.
    What shall the tariff be?
    Oh, what shall the tariff be?

                           *—Springfield (Mass.) Union.*

---

## WHEN MY OLD HAT WAS NEW.

When my old hat was new ('twas back in sixty-one),
Brave boys went out to battle and with them Harrison,
They fought for union of the States, for abolition, too,
And many boys were brought home dead, when my old
    hat was new.

When my old hat was new, G. Cleveland was a man,
But he preferred to stay at home, a-playing cards with
　　Dan;
He hired a substitute to fight—that was much safer, too,
And kept one eye on Canada, when my old hat was
　　new.

When my old hat was new, Judge Thurman was at
　　home,
He thought it was a sin to fight—this Roman just from
　　Rome—
Rebellion he considered right, and negro slavery too;
He kissed the hand that struck the flag, when my old
　　hat was new.

When my old hat was new, the friends of liberty
Knew well the merits of young Ben, while fighting at
　　Peach Tree;
Come now, huzza for Harrison, just as we used to do,
When first we heard our country's call, and my old hat
　　was new.

———

## CLEVELAND'S VICE.

AIR—"*Meerchaum Pipe.*"

Oh, who is Grover Cleveland's Vice,
　　Cleveland's Vice,
Oh, who is Grover Cleveland's Vice,
　　Cleveland's Vice,
Oh, who is Grover Cleveland's Vice
　　In this trip up Salt creek?
　　Allen Thurman!

Oh, who is riding on behind?
Allen Thurman!   Red Bandan!

Oh, which of them should ride in front?
Allen Thurman!  Red Bandan!  Old Roman!

Oh, who is being sacrificed?
Allen Thurman!  Red Bandan!  Old Roman!  That is the
    plan!

Oh, whose life will ambition cost?
Allen Thurman!  Red Bandan!  Old Roman!  That is the
    plan!  Devised by Dan!  BAD MAN!!

---

## SET HIM THERE K–SOCK.

And they's still another idy 'at I ort to here append,
In a sort o' nota beany, fer to taper off the end,
In a manner more befittin' to a subject jes' in view,
Regardin' things in politics, and what we're goin' to do.

Along a little later, when affairs at Washington,
'At's been harassin' us so long, has got so Harrison,
We're goin' to give the man a seat, and set him there
    k–sock,
When the frost is on the punkin and the fodder's in the
    shock.
                    — *James Whitcomb Riley.*

## OUR OWN PUBLICATIONS.